INTRODUCTION TO STARLIGHT (Ages 7-12)

Starlight is a book for children aged 7-12 who have a parent with a serious illness, such as cancer. It's a story of a life-changing event that happens to Lucas as he lives in a magical land with lots of other families and children, 'just like you' and about the emotional impact this has and how he deals with it.

Readers have the opportunity to relate to Lucas as 'our friend'; at many points in the story; 'and that boy at the table – he looks just like you,' and later, 'and he sounds like you, too.'

The story focuses on uninvited change, the shock of how life becomes 'strange' and how Lucas has to adapt, without knowing how or what to. The unfamiliarity of hospitals and medics is portrayed through the positive lens of hope 'they're warriors with wings.'

It provides readers with the ability to relate to changes in family life: 'She looks different, sounds different, even smells different,' whilst 'Dad's burnt dinner.' It also highlights the various feelings in the family as illness progresses. 'I can't stand this!' shouts Dad, whilst Lucas 'throws away the sun' and worries whether it's his fault she's sick.

Through the use of stars, our friend is able to identify the many fe[...] for example that wo[...] hand and contradictorily, so do happy and guilty. With the help of an angry but magical dragon who provides a stone to keep safe and the lighting of stars in a sky dark through the loss of the sun, our friend is able to reconnect with people important to him.

This book is ideal to help children aged 7-12 express their feelings and worries about a loved one who has a serious illness such as cancer, as well as express their confusion and anger at the changes that occur within the family. It highlights the importance of recognising emotions as well as the healing power of expressing them, whatever they are. It conveys a sad but realistic message that even in the absence of a power to heal, our emotions are uplifting and connect you to the people you love, because in the absence of the sun there is still hope in the light of the stars if you find your way to reach out to them.

Sincerely,
Dr Nihara Krause,
MSc, PsychD, C.Psychol, CSci, AFBPsS
Consultant Clinical Psychologist

For my children and my husband;
"But surely we are brave"

Lara

There are many loved ones I would love to dedicate this book to, but no one more so than my beloved mother Anni, who is battling cancer while we are finishing this book. Originally, I wanted to be a part of this project to have a book for my own children while I was sick. During this process, however, I realised that it was myself who had became the child, as I was filled with guilt and darkness; a numbness of pain and an overwhelming fear of losing my own beloved mother.

Anni, my beautiful mother, I hope you will understand how much I love you, how much you mean to me, and how much you have inspired me all throughout my life.

X Line

Welcome! Welcome
to the Enchanted Forest,
Where twinkling fairies fly
right past your face!
Ride flame-breathing dragons,
spot rare unicorns
This forest is truly a magical place!

Come along! Climb aboard the 213 Dragon!
He's faster than travelling by bus or by rail
But careful- he's grumpy and often breathes fire
At children who poke him or stand on his tail.

Strap on your
seatbelts,
hold tight
and let's go!
Watch the
twinkling life
of the forest fly by!

We're off on a wild and
life-changing journey
Which you cannot predict,
nor understand why.

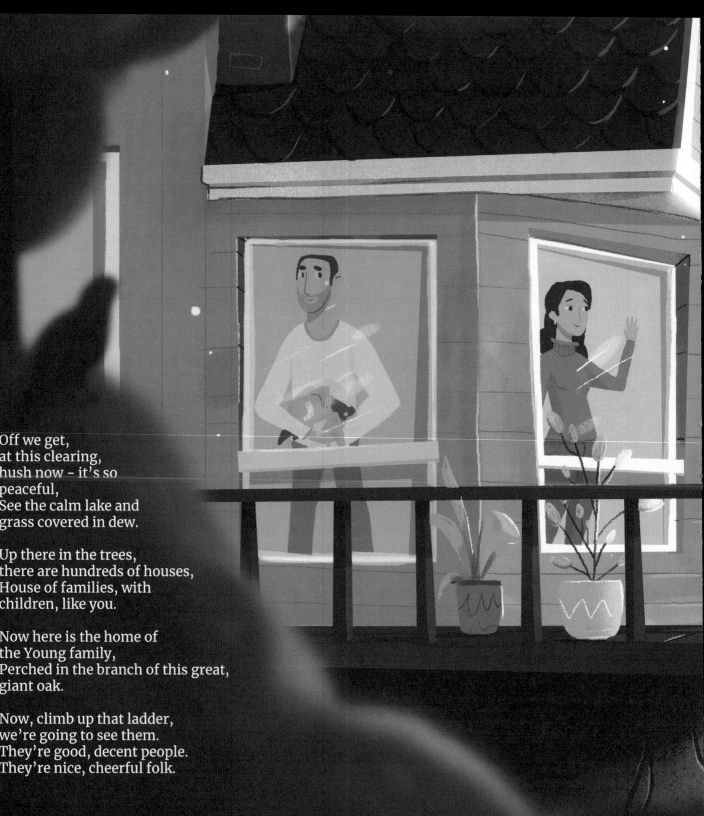

Off we get,
at this clearing,
hush now – it's so
peaceful,
See the calm lake and
grass covered in dew.

Up there in the trees,
there are hundreds of houses,
House of families, with
children, like you.

Now here is the home of
the Young family,
Perched in the branch of this great,
giant oak.

Now, climb up that ladder,
we're going to see them.
They're good, decent people.
They're nice, cheerful folk.

They're clearing their plates,
grabbing shoes, bags and coats,
And that boy at the table–
he looks just like you!
His name is Lucas
and he's leaving for school now,
"Bye Mum! Bye Dad!"
And he sounds like you, too!

The days have their patterns,
weeks have their routines,
They're all just fine thanks,
they don't want change.
But change, it is coming,
and no-one can stop it.
Life, for this family
is about to get strange.

Our friend's home from school,
he calls "thanks!" to the dragon,
He plays with his friends in the warm, summer air.
But watch how leaves fall, light fades, wind blows,
Silence approaches and winter is near.

Here is change. It has come.
Though it was not invited.
Mum is unwell.
She's tired and worn out.
Our friend must be brave now,
without knowing how to.
But he'll learn of course,
as he's strong inside-out.

Our friend nods, Dad nods,
Mum tries to smile.
Mum's very sick,
what more can they say?
They try to ignore it,
they try to talk over it.
But it's there in the room.
It won't go away.

The dragon is quiet as
they travel together
To hospital, where you see
all sorts of things,
Like fairies who work their magic all day
And all night, without rest;
they're warriors with wings.

And look! Over there! The unicorns are coming!
See their sharp, pointed horns;
their imposing physique;
Their white coats a uniform
Of an army which fight
On behalf of the needy,
the sick and the weak.

Watch how they roll out
maps of the body
Saying, "There it is, look!
X marks the spot."
They have powers so great
we forget they are mortal,
But these mortals
are simply the best hope we've got.

Mum stays behind
and the others go home.
Dad's grumpy, he shouts,
he makes quite a row.
Our friend stomps to his room;
he feels so alone.
Because Mum is the one who
needs all the hugs now.

Mum's home!
Our friend leaps up with excitement.
But she seems so frail he fears she might break.
She looks different,
sounds different,
even smells different.
All night he's exhausted, but all night he's awake.

His teachers don't mind if he forgets his homework.
At school, he still likes to laugh
with his friends.
It's confusing because some days he feels happy,
While at home Dad complains,
"this nightmare won't end."

Dad's burnt dinner,
but they don't feel like eating.
"I can't stand this!" He shouts,
"I can't do it! I'm done!"
Mum's looking pale
and Dad's feeling awful.
They've all had enough.
Hang on- wait-
where's Lucas gone?

Quick, let's find him!
Out the house, down the tree.
He's there, watching the sun
as it pulls down the day.
But he's grabbed it!
He's thrown the sun at the treehouse!
Lucas,
that won't make
mum's illness go away!

Oh look.
The sky's gone black.

Dad stomps down the ladder, carrying the sun like a ball.
"Are you mad?" He shouts, as Lucas shakes his head.
Dad sighs, plays with the ball in his hand
And says with a sigh, "Was it something I said?"

"Sometimes I think that it's my fault she's sick."
Lucas reveals quietly while starting to cry.
"I know it's not true, but it makes me think
That if I can control it, it means she won't die!"

"Will I get sick too?" Now he looks panicked,
"I don't want to catch it, I don't want to be ill!"
Dad says,
"It is not your fault and you cannot catch it.
But will she get better? I don't know if she will."

"Sometimes
I think
that it's my
fault..."

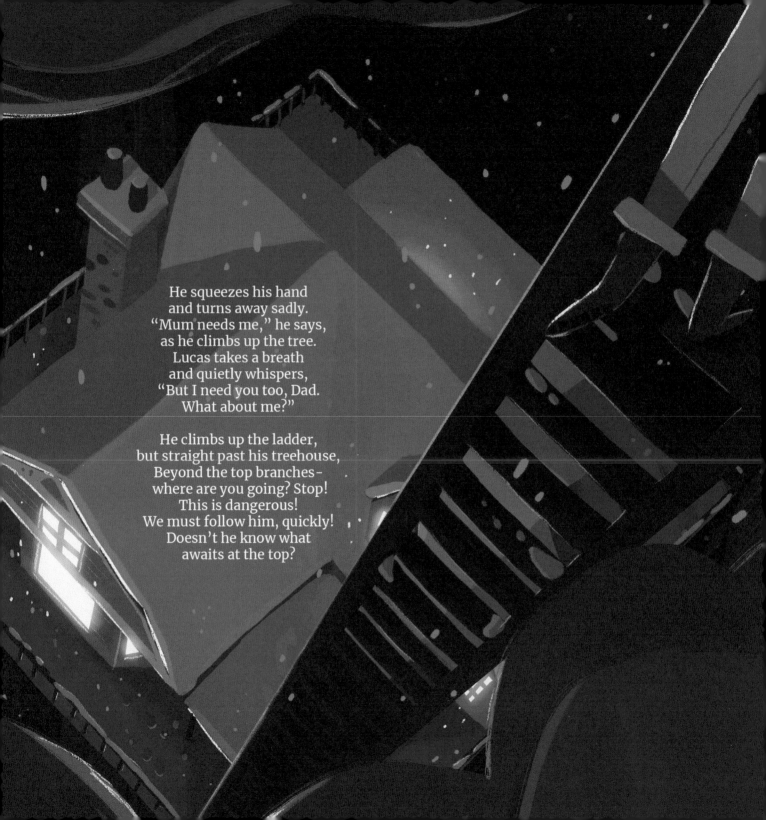

He squeezes his hand
and turns away sadly.
"Mum needs me," he says,
as he climbs up the tree.
Lucas takes a breath
and quietly whispers,
"But I need you too, Dad.
What about me?"

He climbs up the ladder,
but straight past his treehouse,
Beyond the top branches –
where are you going? Stop!
This is dangerous!
We must follow him, quickly!
Doesn't he know what
awaits at the top?

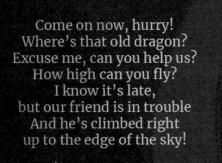

Come on now, hurry!
Where's that old dragon?
Excuse me, can you help us?
How high can you fly?
I know it's late,
but our friend is in trouble
And he's climbed right
up to the edge of the sky!

And beyond the sky is a night
filled with darkness,
For the moon lost the sun
which acts as it's guide,
And in darkness is fear,
where monsters are lurking,
That feed off the terror
that's trapped deep inside.

"I feel SO alone ..."

There he is! Sitting cross-legged on a cloud while darkness creeps in; he's engulfed by the night. He looks lost, he looks scared, he begins to look panicked – we must help him! Our hero's not ready to fight! Lucas, are you anxious? You must say what you feel! As he fights off the darkness, he lets out a groan. But Lucas, can you hear us? Describe your emotions! A tiny voice whispers, "I feel so alone."

One star starts to shine.
It's tiny but glowing.
That star creates light,
and Lucas, it's yours now.
It's hard to accept your feelings,
but touch them,
Explore them, and slowly,
you'll understand how.

"I feel worried," he says
and another lights up.
And another, because worried
and sad are a pair.
As he pulls the two stars together,
tears fall,
Making light pour in
droplets down from the air.

"Sometimes I'm happy
and it makes me feel guilty!
But now it makes sense
that happy's not wrong.
And I'm so angry too!
Because none of it's fair!"
And the light from
three more stars glows strong.

He continues his quest of
exploring his feelings,
The terror grows weak as
he conquers the night.
"I feel so many things
and they're all so important."

Well done, Lucas.

You've nailed it.

The sky fills with starlight.

He reaches, sweeps
the stars into his hands,
As he looks at his palms,
the light makes his face glow,
He pauses then blows
the stars back to the sky,
He smiles for a moment,
then looks down below.

The dragon flies over
and plucks out a star,
Whispers, "Lucas,
I know you've struggled to cope."
With flaming breath
he turns the star to a stone,
And says,
"You can keep this one.
I've called it hope."

Lowering his wings
for our friend to climb on,
The dragon flies us all
back down through the air.
From this day forward,
if our friend needs comfort,
He'll hold his stone tight
and know that it's there.

Back in the treehouse, Mum's lying down, resting.

Dad plays with the sun in his hand, like a ball.
Then he places it back at the edge of the world.

And as the sun rises up,
the night starts to fall.

Clouds part, the sun shines
and the animals wake up,
Small shoots start to grow,
blossom blooms from the tree,
Children frolic and play
down in the fresh grass,
Lucas takes a deep breath
and calls ...

"Hey! Wait for me!"

Now, the stars in this
forest have marvellous powers,
But I'm sorry to say,
not the power to heal.
They can't make Mum better,
but they'll teach you things
By helping you accept
the way that you feel.

That completes your tour
of the forest, my friend!
A magical place filled
with wondrous delight!
But, remember, as you go
home to fight your own battles,
You have the power
to make your own starlight.

PARENTS' GUIDE BY DR KRAUSE

Supporting children's emotions when a parent has a serious illness such as cancer needs multiple sources of help since a parent's serious illness is one of the most difficult challenges a child can face. Stories can be a useful way for children to have feelings validated, know that they are not alone and learn how to express difficult emotions safely. It can also provide focus as a family activity and help at a time when explaining the illness seems overwhelmingly hard.

When a parent is seriously ill, it is not unusual for life at home to change overnight. Dealing with a serious illness can often preoccupy an adult's thoughts and this, together with the wide range of emotions felt can make it hard to connect to children's needs, which are often not that obvious. This can be similar for the parent who is well and who has their own feelings to deal with, the need to support their partner's fears and worries as well as caring for their health, navigate the practicalities of medical appointments and treatment as well as balance day-to-day responsibilities and work.

How children respond to such an event will depend, amongst other factors, on their age and developmental level, their personality, the family structure and coping style, as well as the other difficult experiences they have experienced. Psychological literature indicates that traumatic experiences – both 'big' and 'small' add up, increasing anxiety. If one of these experiences is of a family member who had cancer, this can be confusing and frightening, especially if the person has died. In addition children who are already vulnerable to stressors, such as, for example, children with pre-existing anxiety conditions, depression or neurodevelopmental conditions such attention deficit disorder may need extra support to cope with this challenge. Yet being able to have a trusted adult in their lives, ways of making themselves feel safe, known routines and most importantly, the on-going opportunity to express and be validated for whatever feelings they have, creates safety and helps deal with the experiences they are going through.

A child's developmental stage plays a key role in how they are able to understand and cope with the parent' illness. Being aware of these stages can help to distinguish the difficulties related to the impact of the parent's illness from normal developmental challenges and also know the most effective ways to support them.

Infants and Toddlers (0-2 years)

This group of children are sensitive to changes in routine and changes in caregivers. They will not be able to understand or appreciate the concept of a serious illness. They will, however, pick up on parent/caregiver emotions and often mirror them. They are most likely to show their distress through behaviours such as becoming increasingly clingy, fussy over things they weren't before, refusing well-established sleep and eating routines, shifting to 'younger' behaviours such as wanting the bottle rather than solids. Delay may be noted in speech and steps to independence. Keeping routines as similar as possible, having known carers, delaying toilet training if distress is shown, maintaining boundaries over bedtimes, accepting that tantrums may be increased and an expression of distress rather than behaviour to be tamed and consistent and increased affection will help soothe the distress caused by the changes being experienced.

Pre and early school (3-6 years)

Children of this age will lack the cognitive understanding required to appreciate the details of a serious illness. Due to their stage of thinking being related to personal cause and effect it is not uncommon for children of this age to misunderstand the cause of the illness and blame themselves. Repeated explanations may help, always taking care to take away any worry or blame they may have. Increased sensitivity to what's happening around them will be common – so expect a much bigger emotional reaction to things. They may also lapse into 'younger' behaviours such as bedwetting for example, or have frequent 'toddler tantrums.' Others may withdraw and be quiet and subdued. Permitting the expression of emotions, immediate loving care and soothing and increased tactile comfort will be helpful. This group will also be sensitive to changes in routine and may push boundaries or show distress. Death is often seen as reversible by this age group so they will not be able to easily respond to change that is permanent in advance. This group of children benefit from being able to express their emotions through play since verbal expression of emotions is difficult.

Mid-school (7-12 years)

This is a difficult age to learn about serious illness for a number of reasons. Firstly, the concept of death being permanent starts around this age making young people of this age anxious about loss. Secondly it's a time when a sense of identity is starting to form and peer relationships become extremely important. Young people of this age can become very conscious of themselves and can also become easily embarrassed or worried about others' evaluation or judgement of them. Whilst they will understand the concept of a serious illness they are likely to worry about how this will affect their peers' acceptance of them. Will they be different, for example? This may lead to not wanting to share what's happening with others and of trying to contain emotions. These emotions will most likely be expressed through behaviours such as irritability or anger or through sadness and anxiety. They may also fear the illness being contagious, and may show this behaviourally – for example, increased hand washing, by not wanting to be near medical professionals or hospitals or by avoiding the unwell parent. Gently making sure they face these fears is a good step forward. Occasionally these fears may be shown either as health related anxiety or with increasing physical complaints. They may also feel unnecessary guilt about causing pain or harm to the parent who has the serious illness and worry about whether they have contributed to or caused the illness through their behaviour. Possible school changes and academic pressures towards the end of this time period can also cause distress. For some children school can become a refuge - the structure and routine providing a known familiarity that is comforting as well as a distraction from home,

which may be distressing. For others however, it may become a challenge, impacting on behaviour at school, schoolwork and friendships. If any peers have had experiences with cancer or other serious illnesses, which they share with the child, this can also cause increased anxiety. Engaging school in supporting the young person, having a teacher or older student who they can go to if distressed at school and having a comforter from home such as a book, blanket, toy in their school bag can help. This group responds well to written material, stories, films, expressing their feelings through talking, writing, music, art or acting.

Adolescents (13-18 years)

This is a very tricky age to experience a serious illness in a parent. Adolescents will be able to understand details of the diagnosis together with the outcome. They may often look up symptoms and prognoses online, and access on-line support in preference to face-to-face support due to anonymity. Those adolescents who find it easier to express how they feel may turn to friends or other family members but most commonly they will withdraw from showing their feelings, either to protect others around them or because they don't want to show their upset. Some may engage in risk-taking behaviours, disengage from schoolwork, withdraw from friends or become extra clingy. Some will find it easier to tolerate uncertainty than others but in general they will find the lack of certainty stressful and this will be shown in their behaviours, usually shown through increased irritation and anger. Since the adolescent brain is developing, some young people may not be able to show the empathy or adaptation necessary to accommodate for family change. This apparent 'selfishness' can often make parents feel upset or angry at a time when everyone is feeling stretched and kindness and consideration is of value. Rather than expecting adolescents to be instinctively responsive, it may be helpful to provide them with expected changes, keep up open and honest communication about the condition, set up one to one times to do an activity together which also provides an opportunity to talk, inform school of the circumstances at home and encourage supportive friends and family to engage with providing extra support.

Perhaps what's most important when a parent has a serious illness is for all concerned to develop ways to build their resilience to dealing with what they are facing. With this in mind, keep the child or young person's feelings central and provide them with opportunities to communicate what they are feeling and make sure they are heard. Convey confidence in their ability to deal with change and be mindful of your emotional responses. Draw upon as much support as is available so that there is a 'resilience boosting team' and strategies around the family which includes books, films, on-line resources, friends, family, teachers and, if helpful, therapists. Prepare children and young people as well as yourself for what needs to be faced. Preparation, even if it's for a difficult outcome, helps reduce anxiety, enables connection and generates alternative and positive ways of dealing with pain. Being honest and open about the situation and helping children and young people find their own strengths through expressing what they feel and learning how to deal with these feelings provides them with resilience to deal with uncertainty and change.

Dr Nihara Krause
MSc, PsychD, C.Psychol, CSci, AFBPsS
Consultant Clinical Psychologist

Firstly, a big thank you to our team of psychologists who volunteered their time and energy to help us ensure this is book is a genuine, well-researched and quality-assured resource for children and families. Dr Nihara Krause, Consultant Clinical Psychologist and Author of *Outside In*, and Dr Stephanie Satariano, Educational Psychologist in Paediatric Neuropsychology, who between them dedicated many hours to this project, making suggestions, inputting ideas and explaining the varied psychological aspects of youth mental health from their respective fields, as well as providing much insight on our videos. Dr Genevieve von Lob, Clinical Psychologist and Author of *Five Deep Breaths: The Power of Mindful Parenting*, who carefully reviewed the book and Journalist and Author of *Aftershock*, Matthew Green, both of whom consistently responded to my queries about mental health and PTSD. Special thanks goes to Dr Krause, who also wrote the Introduction and Parents' Manual for *Starlight*, and who continues to do inspirational work with her youth mental health charity, Stem4.

Finally, we would like to thank you for reading *Starlight* and we hope that you have learnt much from Lucas's tale of true courage. We would love to hear your feedback, so please drop us a message on *Facebook* or *Instagram*.

Love Lara & Line

Printed in Great
Britain
by Amazon